KT-468-838

"Is it yes?"

"Uh… no!"

"Let's try an easier one...

What's the opposite of up?"

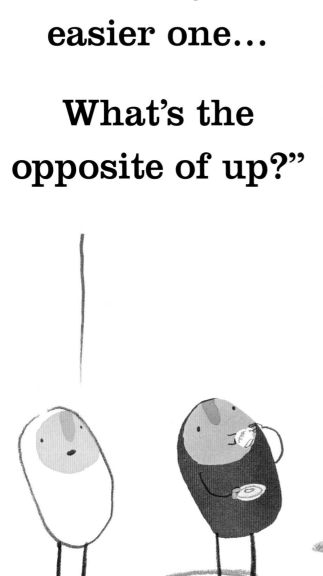
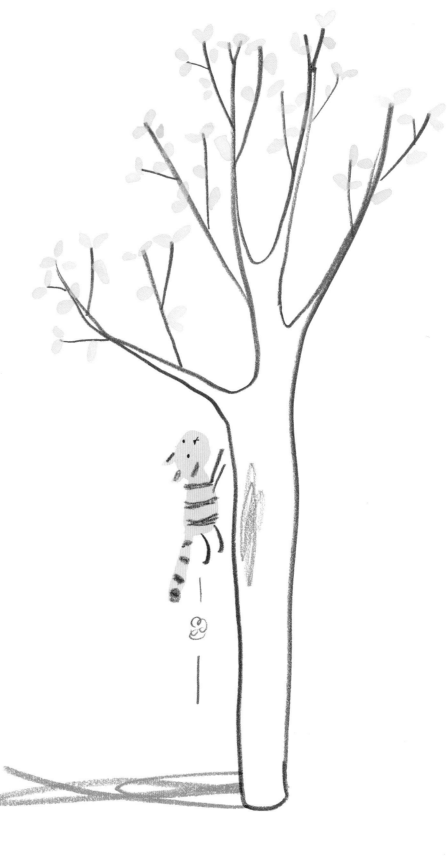

The HUEYS in WHAT's the OPPOSITE?

WITHDRAWN FROM STOCK

OLIVER JEFFERS

 HarperCollins *Children's Books*

And the opposite of high...

Here...

and there!"

"There…

and here?"

"Now you've got it!
How about a few more?

Cold...   hot.

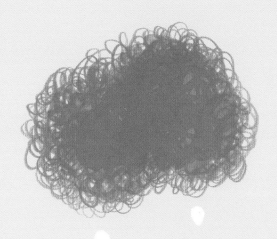

Unlucky...

lucky…

unlucky again.

On...

off.

Big…

small.

Light...

heavy.

Happy…

sad.

Now for a trickier one...

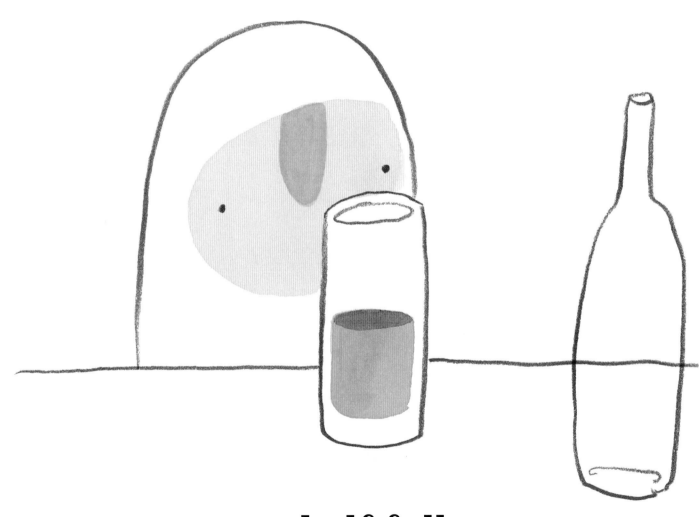

half full

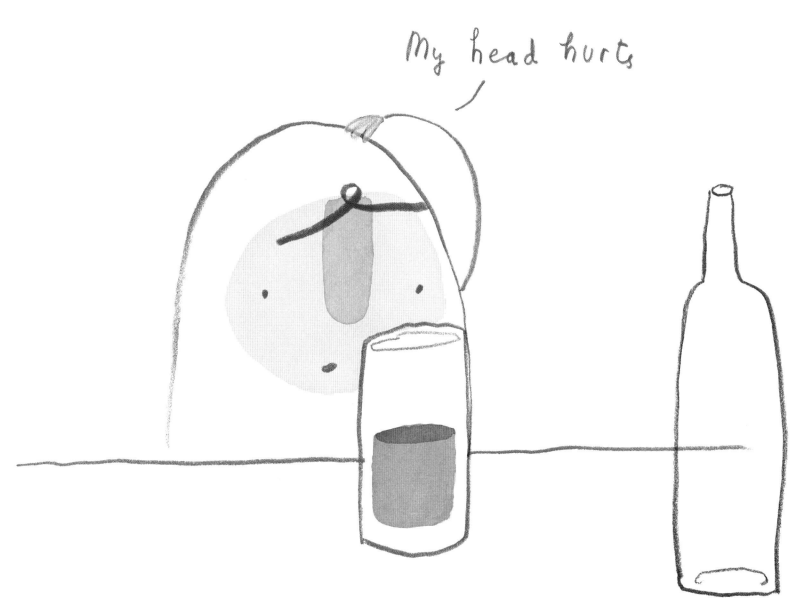

half empty.

All right, let's finish with something simple..."

BACK!

"So…
what IS the opposite
of the beginning?"

"Oh, yes!
It's…